Ordinary Mary's

I think you're great!

Positively Extraordinary Day

MANUFACTURED IN CHINA AUGUST 2019, BY TOPPAN PRINTING CO. LTD.

FIRST EDITION
23 22 21 20 19   5 4 3 2 1

PUBLISHED BY
GIBBS SMITH
P.O. BOX 667
LAYTON, UTAH 84041

ORDERS: 1 (800) 835–4993

WWW.GIBBS–SMITH.COM

DESIGNED BY NICOLE LARUE

GIBBS SMITH BOOKS ARE PRINTED ON EITHER RECYCLED, 100% POST–CONSUMER WASTE, FSC–CERTIFIED PAPERS OR ON PAPER PRODUCED FROM SUSTAINABLE PEFC–CERTIFIED FOREST/CONTROLLED WOOD SOURCE. LEARN MORE AT WWW.PEFC.ORG.

LIBRARY OF CONGRESS CONTROL NUMBER: 2018968415

ISBN: 978–1–4236–5181–9

Ordinary Mary's

Positively Extraordinary Day

BY EMILY PEARSON ILLUSTRATIONS BY FUMI KOSAKA

GIBBS SMITH
TO ENRICH AND INSPIRE HUMANKIND

For Mister Rogers. Thank you. — E. P.

For Kenji and Izumi — F. K.

Ordinary Mary was very ordinary, even though she had once changed the world. This girl? Yes, this girl! She had once changed the world.

And she's about to do it again.

One ordinary day, skipping to her ordinary bus stop, on her way to her ordinary school, Mary passed the ordinary bushes she passed every other day, and picked a sunflower and continued on her way.

On the bus there was a fuss with a not-very-nice kid named John.
He thought it was funny to tease Mia, a girl whose clothes were
old and didn't fit quite right.

"Look," John pointed and laughed.
"There's a great big hole in your shoe!"

Mary spoke up and said to Mia. "I think you look nice and I really like your hair."
Mary handed Mia the sunflower, and then she smiled at John. "And I like your backpack."

"Yeah, your backpack is cool," said Kenji. "And if I could throw a football like you, maybe I'd get picked for a team too."

John's teasing stopped. And thanks to Mary, every kid on the bus suddenly felt brave. Maybe they too could find a friend to defend and help others have a happier day.

One of those kids was Chris, who, now feeling brave, gave a friendly wave and said "thank you" to Gus, who drove the big bus.

No one had ever thanked Gus before. He was so pleased, that he smiled a smile as wide as a mile and said, "Hey kid, make it a good day."

What? A good day is something you can choose? That new thought made Chris so excited he couldn't wait to help other kids choose a good day too.

One of those kids was Lucia, who was struggling to get her heavy school project out of the car.

Chris beamed as he helped Lucia carry her project to class. That turned Lucia's mood right around and she said to herself, "Maybe my load isn't as heavy as I thought."

All at once her shoulders felt lighter and her heart felt brighter. And that made her want to lighten the load of other kids too.

One of those kids was Aman, who sat in a slump and seemed down in the dumps. Lucia passed him a note that said "I think you're great!"

And just like that, Aman sat up straighter and took a deep breath and felt better. Four simple words that he hardly ever heard made all the difference.

Mr. Jenkins noticed too. When he saw the words on Lucia's note, and the difference they made, he had an idea.

Each kid in the class would write a positive note and pass it on to another kid at the assembly that morning.

Oh, how great! The kids couldn't wait!

One by one the kids handed out their notes, and as they did, every heart got happier and every smile got bigger.

The principal, Ms. Thomas, saw the happiness spread and was delighted with what the notes said.

As she left the assembly, Ms. Thomas saw Lucas, Ava, and Noah, each with mischief in their eye. They had all spent time in her office for making other kids cry.

Inspired, she smiled and said, "Our school is filled with kids who are lonely and scared. It would be great if they knew that somebody cared. Would you be willing to lend a hand?"

"Sure," Ava shrugged. "I guess we could try."

So, Ms. Thomas gave them each a special badge. "You're on patrol at recess today as the Kindness Crew. I'm counting on you to make the playground a safe and happy place."

That was the first time those kids left her office walking tall. With heads held high, they joined the other kids in the hall.

One of those
kids was Sam, who
was so overjoyed from getting
a note that he had to do something
to help others feel the same. He gave a
big smile to Betty the lunch lady, who usually
frowned a whole bunch, and actually said "please" when
he asked for his lunch.

That turned Betty's frown right upside down. "You're the first one to say 'please.'"
The next kid overheard and also said "please." And the next one did too, and the one
after that. And for each smile she got, Betty gave a smile right back.

Each of those kids carried trays with heaping helpings of happy.

One of those kids was Tara, who was eating lunch with her friends. She noticed a girl at the next table pretending it didn't matter that she was alone.

Well, it mattered to Tara. She was up like a shot.

"Hi, I'm Tara. Would you like to eat lunch with us?"

"I'm Kali." The girl's face lit up. "Thanks, I would like that a lot."

Other kids noticed and did the same, and soon not one single kid in the lunchroom was eating alone.

When Kali played with her new friends, she felt cared for and cheerful and didn't want those good feelings to end.

As she ran past John, the not-so-nice kid on her bus who liked to tease, she slipped him a note and gave his hand a squeeze.

"Someone thinks you're great."

John couldn't believe these words he read over and over. He was great? He'd never heard that before. But, boy, he sure liked how it felt.

After recess, it was time for math—and John hated math.

But that day, with that note in his pocket, a brand-new feeling became a brand-new thought:

"I wonder what would happen if I gave it a shot?"

For the first time, John tried hard with the rest of the class. And—you guessed it—he actually passed!

After school, the same kids waited for the same bus, but this day something was different.

"Hey," John said to Mia. "Sorry I was mean this morning. Who cares if there's a hole in your shoe?"

Then he smiled at Kenji. "You said my backpack was cool— and it has a hole in it too."

Then John tossed a football to Kenji and taught him how to throw like a pro. Kenji was so happy that he decided to help others feel happy too.

Not one kid was frowning, not one kid was sad. Everyone got on the bus feeling grateful and glad.

Back at school, the Kindness Crew knocked on the principal's door.

"It felt cool to protect the school," they said. "Can we keep our badges and maybe earn a few more?"

As Lucas, Ava, and Noah left school, they saw Kalea, who had just missed her bus. Noah asked kindly, "Would you like to walk home with us?"

Kalea was so grateful that she decided to make other kids feel included and a lot less alone.

One was a girl sitting on the curb looking sad.

"Hi," Kalea said.
"Is it okay if I sit down?"

The girl looked up and said with a frown, "Yeah, I just got some sad news today. My very best friend is moving away."

"I just moved here." Kalea's voice was kind. "And I had to leave my very best friend behind. My name is Kalea."

"Hi, Kalea," the girl started to smile. "My name is Mary. Sure, you can sit here a while."

Mary? Ordinary Mary? Yes, it was true! A day that had begun with her being a friend ended with her finding a new one too.

And what's more, Mary's courage and kindness had spread all day long, reaching farther than she could ever have imagined.

Every kid (and grownup) who felt happy, cared for, and strong made others feel safe, loved, and like they belonged.

Feelings that good were too hard to hold in. They spilled out of cars and homes and flooded the streets— they even went global in chats, posts, and tweets.

That night, in a million different places, grateful heads rested on pillows and smiles lingered on faces.

All because—and I promise it's true—one very ordinary day, one very ordinary girl made a choice that was extraordinarily positive and positively extraordinary.

And, you know what? I bet you could too!